JUST *Gotta* SAY

NEW YORK TIMES BESTSELLING AUTHOR
LAURA KAYE

OTHER BOOKS BY LAURA KAYE

Hearts of the Anemoi Series
NORTH OF NEED
WEST OF WANT
SOUTH OF SURRENDER
EAST OF ECSTASY
HEARTS OF THE ANEMOI BOX SET

Vampire Warrior Kings Series
IN THE SERVICE OF THE KING
SEDUCED BY THE VAMPIRE KING
TAKEN BY THE VAMPIRE KING
VAMPIRE WARRIOR KINGS BOX SET

Hard Ink Series
HARD AS IT GETS
HARD AS YOU CAN
HARD TO HOLD ON TO
HARD TO COME BY
HARD TO BE GOOD
HARD TO LET GO

CHAPTER ONE

Callie Davis was thrilled to find herself home alone on a Saturday night. With her three roommates—Lucas, Jack, and Noah—gone to a baseball game, she was free to try all those naughty, nasty things she'd been burning to do ever since she'd walked down the night-darkened hallway and witnessed Jack and Noah tangled together in bed.

Hypnotized by the unexpected sight of the two men loving each other, she'd stared for untold minutes through the not-quite-shut door. Jack Fenton and Noah Ryder were big guys and had been no-holds-barred all over each other. Visions of groping hands, aggressive kisses, and pistoning hips tormented her. The sounds they'd made taunted her just as much—Jack's needy curses and encouragements, Noah's guttural moans, their frantic breathing. Remembering made her instantly wet.

Each night since, she'd given in to the ache, her own fingers a poor substitute for her imaginings of how the guys' thick fingers and thicker cocks would feel. She'd never before been aroused by the idea of being with more than one lover. Now, the simple thought of it got her off faster than anything ever had.

But damn, as good as the fantasizing was, it wasn't enough. Callie needed more.

Entering her small, second-floor bedroom, she switched on the glass desk lamp and cued up the "Sexy Times" playlist on her iPod. She let one suggestive tune after another soak in and bolster her conviction to give her plan a try. She shed her clothes in a messy pile at the foot of her narrow bed and slipped into a short, hot pink silk robe. At the edge of her closet, she dropped onto her knees, the plush carpeting providing a cushion. Nearly giddy with excitement, she yanked a bag from behind a crate of shoes.

Just yesterday, she'd passed that funky little sex shop near Dupont Circle, and an idea popped into her mind, opening up a much-needed path to a more satisfying release. She'd noticed the store before though never patronized it, but the depth of her horniness demanded she suck up her fear and go inside. *Sometimes you just gotta say 'what the fuck.'*

What the fuck, indeed.

She'd repeated her favorite saying like a mantra as she backtracked down P Street, away from the ever-present D.C. traffic in the Circle, past a used bookstore she loved, to the adult shop nestled between a Chinese restaurant and a delicatessen. The historic building was like so many others in this eclectic neighborhood, where multi-million-dollar mansions housed foreign embassies alongside trendy restaurants and, well, stores like this one. With a deep breath and a rueful grin, she'd jogged up the steps and entered the store, which had been clean, well-lit, and surprisingly busy for a Friday afternoon.

Kneeling on her bedroom floor, she peered into the bag and surveyed her purchases. It contained everything she needed to bring her three-way fantasy to life and then some. The lubricant, big set of anal toys, and double-headed dildo had been must-haves. You could never have too many vibrators, and the purple one she'd found had just been so damn cute. Of course, visual aids were key, so she'd bought a DVD.

Yep. She had everything she needed.

Bag of naughtiness in hand, she jogged downstairs and stopped in the kitchen to pour herself a margarita from the pitcher she'd left chilling in the fridge. Anticipation tingled low in her gut as she entered the den to make use of the 48" plasma. She was going to do this right—hi-def, surround sound, and all.

Callie closed the door and settled her toys on the table. She loaded the DVD, hoping the movie lived up to its ridiculous but promising name: *3-Way-Stravaganza*. On the way to the leather couch she shrugged out of her robe, the blue flickering of the huge television providing the only light. She felt a little foolish until the screen started playing snippets from each of the six scenes against the background of a hot, rhythmic bass beat. Her own pulse matched the music.

Oh, yeah. This would do just fine.

Eyeing the TV, she took a big sip of her frosty drink. The tangy flavor burst on her tongue and added to the heat gathering in her belly. A trio of groans drew her gaze to the television. Watching the threesome writhe on the bed, Callie savored another cold drink of her cocktail. It was time.

She unpacked all the new sex-shop goodies, as well as her trusty pink rabbit. The kinky display covered the coffee table's surface. She bit down on her bottom lip. Where to start?

Mere anticipation made her wet, arousal dampening the skin and fine hair between her legs. Aiming the remote, she selected the first scene. Her heart raced as two men rubbed their hands all over a woman's body. Callie's mind swapped out the actors' features with those of herself and her friends. The man with a big tribal tattoo on his shoulder became Jack, and she could easily see Jack in the guy's desperate, muttered expletives. The second man was quiet, so to Callie, he was Noah, with short brown curls and mocha-colored skin in place of the actor's buzz cut and coppery tan. Callie, of course, was the blonde they shared between them.

Oh, god. When Movie Jack pushed Blondie to her knees and thrust his thick dick in her face, Callie slid her fingers into the moisture fast accumulating between her thighs and eagerly circled her hot, wet pussy. Her breathing became labored and saliva pooled on her tongue at the thought of the real Jack and Noah panting and grunting while she alternated sucking their cocks, even trying to fit both into her mouth at once. She imagined how her apparently bi boys would moan in pure ecstasy as their cocks rubbed together inside her.

Gaze focused on the screen, Callie gulped another big swallow of margarita before picking up the new double-headed dildo and licking and nibbling at it. The length of rubber fell on her bare breast, the weighty sensation so dirty, so decadent. She rolled it against one nipple, setting off sparks that ricocheted down her body.

The actors' strained sounds filled the dim room, luring her gaze back to the screen. Callie sucked the toy harder. Movie Jack fucked the woman's mouth, the aggressive strokes he delivered pushing down into her throat. Movie Noah crouched behind the woman, his hands groping her breasts while he ground his long dick between her ass cheeks.

Inspired, Callie set the dildo aside and grabbed a softly pointed, medium-sized anal toy. She slathered lube on it and wiped the excess over her rear opening. Reclining against the supple leather of the sofa, she propped her feet on the coffee table to open herself for the plug. With a groan of pure pleasure, she slipped the tip of the clear silicone into her ass just as Movie Noah impaled the actress.

The slick intrusion drew a low hum from Callie's throat. The stretching pressure enflamed her nerves and quivered through her thighs. She'd used her fingers there before, but never anything else. She pushed the toy in farther and sucked in a breath, the delicious sensation of fullness setting her blood ablaze. *God, to do this with the guys for real...*

Callie panted, rolled her hips, and trained her gaze on the shifting scenes before her. Seeking every new feeling she could, she alternated between vibrators and anal playthings. Her arousal spiked at the scene where Movie Jack strapped the woman's back to his chest with his big arms and filled her ass with his cock while Movie Noah took her pussy. She imagined the two men being able to feel one another's cocks slide and grind within her tight channels, and the idea of their pleasure shoved her toward the edge.

Every time she neared orgasm, she slowed the motion of the toys. Her body pulsed with restrained lust. But this little experiment was so damn good she wanted it to last, wanted an absolutely explosive orgasm out of the deal. Since the guys wouldn't be home for hours, she was in no rush.

As the scene changed again, Callie's heart thundered. The scent of her cream swirled in the air as she fucked herself with the new vibrator and pictured Jack's tongue lapping up everything she gave him just as the actor did. Callie's oldest fantasy came to mind then and latched on tight. While none of the scenes featured more than two guys with a woman, she began writing in a role for a third man. And those were the images that made her juices flow the hardest and her orgasm approach like a freaking freight train. Movie Jack and Movie Noah just weren't complete without Movie Lucas—the long-time source of all her orgasmic dreams before her accidental voyeurism.

Lucas Branson, whose broad shoulders, big hands, and too-infrequent smiles owned her. He had short, brown hair that curled at the ends when he let it grow, the most masculine and perpetually stubbled square jaw, and hazel eyes that reflected the anguish he carried inside. She'd never known anyone who looked so tough and serious on the outside, but was so broken-up and vulnerable on the inside. Sometimes her arms ached from the need to hold him, and she couldn't restrain herself. She'd hug him and make a joke about it or roll her eyes like it was no big deal. No, nothing was complete without Lucas.

But despite the four of them living together the past three years, nothing had ever really happened between them. All three men were hot as fuck and smart and funny. Great guys. As her best friends, they would do anything for her, though they treated her like a little sister. Even Lucas, much to her heartache and frustration.

"Damn." Callie sighed at her thoughts and the turn of events on-screen. Both men fucked the woman's pussy, their big, wet cocks rubbing together, their fingers joined in flicking and circling the woman's clit. With each desperate thrust, every pleasured grunt, Callie's orgasm threatened to erupt, the swirling heat within her jangling and intensifying. God, the thought of being able to handle all of her men like that. The woman screamed and thrashed, earning guttural moans and appreciative expletives from low in the men's throats. In turn, they pulled out and sprayed their cum on her body. The man on top covered her ass cheeks in thick, white stripes. The man underneath shot all over her drenched pussy while he stroked himself. The act was so damn primal and sexy that Callie's pussy quivered, tightened.

Just the thought of her men literally falling apart on her, *because* of her...

Callie paused the movie, and with a shaky hand grabbed her margarita. Drained it. Warmth curled through her chest as she licked the sweet drops from her lips. Then she was right back into the movie, determined to let herself go now. Needing the mind-blowing orgasm her body promised. She knew just what would do it, too—the fantasy of having every one of her openings filled by the three men she loved most. She picked up the double-ended dildo and ran one rubber head through her wet pussy lips. The cool silicone was almost startling against the inferno of her cunt, but she welcomed the sensation as she pushed the long cock into her slick entrance. The full, satisfying penetration forced a groan from her mouth. She'd restrained herself for a while now, and damn, did that thick presence feel good inside, stretching, moving. The length of the dildo made it easy for Callie to relax against the warm sofa as she fucked herself, her thrusts matching the actors'.

This was it. Time to put both heads to use and explore full-out whether this fantasy was something she might want to try for real someday. She lubed the dildo's other red head. Her heart thundered. Sweat broke out across her breasts and along her hairline. She swirled the tip against her anus, already quivering from anticipation. Her orgasm approached, gathering delicious energy that nearly stole her breath.

On screen, the actors positioned their woman so she straddled the first guy, taking his cock into her pussy while the second guy came at her from behind and took her ass. Dirty talk flowed from the two men, ramping up Callie's arousal. Dizzy with lust, sexual greed shot through her and sucked her into the moment.

"Take my cock," Movie Jack demanded in a gruff voice as he slammed into the woman.

Oh, god. Callie would take it. Anywhere. Everywhere. Over and over. With that thought, she pushed the dildo into her tight ass.

CHAPTER TWO

"Why are my roommates such fuckwits?" Jack bit out as he glared at Lucas.

Lucas huffed and glared right back. "Look, I'm sorry. All right? I'll buy the pizza and beer when we get home. And besides, it's not like we can't go to the game tomorrow night."

Jack rolled his eyes. "Damn straight you're buying the grub." He chuckled. Damn if this wasn't so par for the course with them. "I can't believe you messed the dates up. Fuck sake."

Noah guffawed into his hand. "Aw, man. The expressions on your faces when we got there, and the park was all dark. And then Lucas asked that homeless guy where everybody was."

Lucas muttered under his breath, which set Jack to laughing finally.

Remembering the homeless man's answer, Jack imitated his voice: "'Ain't no game tonight, son. But can you spare an old man a few dollars?'"

Noah smacked his knee and doubled over. "And he gave him a twenty!"

"I didn't have anything smaller. Shut up."

"Oh, man. Callie is going to have a field day with this," Jack added through his laughter, already picturing the way her open smile would brighten her beautiful face.

Lucas actually blushed. Jack backed off. They all had a bit of a thing for Callie, always sharing subtle looks when she wore something particularly sexy and commiserating when she went out with some douche bag they agreed was miles beneath her. But Lucas had it the worst. And Jack and Noah knew it.

None of them had ever made a move, though, because she was their friend. Really, the four of them were best friends—had been ever since Callie had carried their asses through two semesters of biology labs their sophomore year. She was brilliant and made kick-ass French toast. And could beat all of them playing Halo.

For his part, Jack had never gone after Callie because he didn't think they'd be compatible. Sexually. He liked it hard and fast and even a little kinky. He'd been bisexual for as long as his body knew what arousal was and regularly enjoyed partners from both teams. But he hadn't known that about Noah until last month when he walked in on Jack making out in their den with a guy he'd picked up at a bar. Noah had exploded, hurt and jealousy emanating from those sweet, golden eyes, and Jack saw it for what it was—Noah was interested in him.

Jack pursued that immediately, completely in lust with Noah's strong, silent demeanor and cute-ass curls. They'd slept together for the first time last weekend. Fucking fantastic was the only way to describe what had happened between them. Being with Noah rattled the ground beneath Jack's feet, and while he didn't know what that meant exactly, Jack hoped last weekend was only the first of many.

Noah's chuckles bubbled up every so often. He shook his head. "Good thing I like you two so much, 'cause you know this shit always seems to happen to us."

Jack nodded and grinned, remembering last summer when they'd traveled to the Blue Ridge Mountains to hike and camp only to discover he'd forgotten the tents. He'd been the one to shoulder the grief that time.

"Hey, Lucas? Why don't you call Callie and let her know we're on the way home. See if she wants us to pick up some dinner for her, too," Noah suggested as they waited for their connecting train.

Lucas scratched at the perpetual scruff on his jaw. "Nah. We know what she always gets. We can surprise her. Besides, you dickheads can just wait 'til we get home to tell her what happened."

Noah grinned as he slapped Lucas's broad back. "Aw, now. It's all good."

Lucas shrugged and chuckled. "It is what it is." He rolled his big shoulders and cracked his neck. The tallest and oldest of the three of them, Lucas still looked like the soldier he'd once been.

Their train breezed into the station and pushed a gust of wind through the cavernous space before coming to a stop. They got on board and found seats.

"What was she doing tonight anyway?" Noah asked.

"She said she didn't have any plans," answered Lucas.

"I think she was just hanging out," Jack said. "Watching movies or something. Probably putting on one of her chick flicks we always bitch about."

Lucas smiled. "Yeah, you always bitch the loudest, Jack, but we all know you love watching that shit with her."

Jack cocked an eyebrow. "Hello, pot, meet kettle." He pushed his shaggy blond hair off his forehead.

"Both of you should just shut the hell up, because you know damn well all three of us would pretty much do anything that girl wanted or asked of us." Noah leveled them with a gaze that dared them to contradict him.

They didn't.

The men sat in silence for a long while, passengers walking between them as they entered and exited at the successive stops. Lucas's troubled sigh finally drew his roommates' gazes.

"Man." Lucas broke the silence and scrubbed his hands over his face. "Where do you think she's gonna land after graduation?"

His buddies issued a collective groan at the question. Callie majored in documentary filmmaking and had offers from jobs and graduate programs in D.C. and New York. Lucas recited prayers nightly that she'd take either the offer from National Geographic or the History Channel, both of which would keep her local. Keep her with them.

With him.

When he and Callie first met three years ago, he'd been such an arrogant prick. You'd never know it by how close they were now. But back then, only a year out of the Army, jaded by the death and destruction he'd witnessed during multiple combat tours, he'd felt ten kinds of derision towards her perfect blonde hair, hip clothes, and purposely shabby messenger bag with all its pins and patches. Damn if he hadn't made a snap judgment, writing her off as knowing a whole lot of nothing about what was real in the world.

When he graduated high school, he hadn't even waited one day, much to his parents' heartbreak, before going down to the recruiting office and signing up. He'd just been restless to *do* something after the attacks of the previous

September. So, after twenty-four months in Iraq, he'd earned that chip on his shoulder honestly. Souvenirs from his time there included the haunting experience of watching one of his best friends die within arm's reach. And then there was the fact that he'd suffered a total loss of hearing in his left ear when the transport he was riding in tripped an IED. The disability prevented him from having any kind of a career in the military.

Not being able to serve carved out the biggest part of that chip, and he'd still been bitter about it when he'd met Callie. Eight weeks into the semester, the four of them had been studying for their first biology midterm. Lucas had showed up late to their study group and hadn't completed his assigned part of the review outline. She'd called him on it, and he'd tossed back some major attitude.

Callie had very calmly passed out the review sheet she'd made for all the guys and packed up her things. Looking down at him, she'd said, "I find it impressive as hell to think, as young as you are, you've done the things you've done and seen the things you've seen. Things that

I'm sure are beyond unimaginable. Things that make the rest of us safe and secure." She'd slung her bag over her shoulder and nailed Lucas with blazing blue eyes.

"But if you think for one minute I'm going to let you treat me like shit for the rest of this semester, you've got another think coming. I've worked damn hard to get where I am. I don't come from a wealthy family. And I'm working two jobs right now to make ends meet. I don't have time for assholes in my life. So, here are your choices: undertake a major fucking attitude adjustment toward me immediately, or one of us is switching out of this study group." Then she'd left.

That was the day Lucas Branson found himself falling in love with Callie Davis.

And in case her words alone hadn't affected the attitude adjustment she'd so courageously demanded, Noah and Jack had ripped him a new one that very night. The fight forged them into best friends. It was the night, over two six packs at Jack's shit-hole apartment, that Lucas had shared with them just a little of his fucked-up combat experience. During that conversation, they'd vowed to make sure no guy ever messed with someone as special as *their* Callie.

So Lucas apologized the next day, earning a beaming smile from her that revealed her obvious relief they could all stay together. Months later, the four of them became roommates—filling up the 20s-era row house in Glover Park where they still lived.

And he'd been falling in love with Callie ever since—which made him terrified he was about to lose her to the brilliant filmmaking career she deserved.

Jack's knee bounced as they sat in silence, his body rocking with the motion of the train. "Man. We need to tell her we want her to stay."

"We can't do that, Jack. She has to do what she wants. Just because we all found jobs or schools here doesn't mean it's best for her." What he didn't say, what he'd never reveal, was that he'd actually passed up a higher-paying job at a New York consulting firm in order to stay in D.C. Near Callie.

Damn, he had it bad.

"He's right," Noah mumbled.

"Fuck," Jack said. "I know."

They got off the metro at Foggy Bottom, right in the heart of George Washington University's hustle and bustle—right where it had all begun for the four of them. Noah and Jack made for the bus stop, but Lucas was suddenly filled with the urge to get home to Callie.

"Hey," he called, "let's take a cab. I just wanna get back. I'll pay."

Jack stepped smoothly out onto 23rd Street and raised his hand. A cab almost immediately stopped, and they piled in. The cabbie pulled a uey that headed them north toward Glover Park.

"Man, if we're not some morose fuckers all of a sudden," Jack muttered.

They all chuckled, and the conversation lightened considerably by the time they emerged from the cab on Wisconsin Avenue to get some dinner and drinks. They split up—Lucas getting the beer, Jack the pizza, and Noah the chocolate ice cream they had to have or Callie would go ballistic. Fifteen minutes later they met to begin the short walk to their place.

Laughing and joking, they jogged up the front steps of the brown brick row house. Noah pushed through the door into the darkened living room and flipped on a light as Jack sang out, "Oh, honey, we're home."

No response.

From the kitchen, where he was stowing the ice cream, Noah called, "Sounds like she's in the den."

That's when Lucas heard it. Rhythmic moans and groans. A female's throaty keening. A man's gruff words: "That's right. You're a little slut, aren't you? Take my cock. Take it!"

The lethal expressions on the other men's faces said they heard it, too.

Lucas was the first to move. "Aw, hell no."

CHAPTER THREE

Callie drew her knees up farther, fucking herself with shallow pumps of the double-headed dildo. Her body relaxed, opened. *Fuck!* She couldn't believe she was doing this, but already a tremendous orgasm gathered in her stomach, thighs, cunt. The actor still spitting out taunts and commands on-screen, Callie heaved a raspy breath and pushed the heads deeper inside her. Good god, if this wasn't the very definition of *sometimes, you just gotta say—*

The door to the den exploded inward, and Lucas skidded into the room, huge shoulders squared off, eyes narrowed, fists clenched. Jack and Noah followed on his heels.

Callie screamed, at first out of genuine fright, and then out of bone-crushing

mortification. Shock froze her for long
seconds, trapping her in a stare-down
with her bewildered roommates. Then
she curled into a ball and groped for her
robe, her hand reaching and searching
before finally, *finally* making contact
with the pink silk. She hauled it over her
body, gripped it tightly to her neck. As
she moved, the dildo slid out of her and
flopped to the floor, which she hoped
with everything she was would open up
and swallow her whole.

"Get out! What are you doing here?
Oh, my god!"

The guys just stood there. Mouths
gaping.   Eyes   flittering   from
embarrassing object to embarrassing
object. The scene on the DVD intensified.
The woman just had to be a fucking
screamer, didn't she?

"Oh, my god. Get out, get out, get out!
Why are you idiots still in here? Get
out!" She pulled the robe over her head,
exposing her thighs. The single coherent
thought she could muster was *oh, my
god*. Over and over.

"Callie—"

"I swear to god..." came her muffled
warning.

Footsteps stumbled against the old hardwood floor. The door clicked shut. The woman screamed again while the men grunted out their orgasms. Still covered by the robe, Callie rolled her eyes.

Oh my fucking god.

In a daze, she eased into a sitting position and jabbed at the remote control until the screen darkened and quieted.

Her gaze moved slowly, as if she were in a dream. Or a nightmare. The coffee table was a veritable cornucopia of sex toys. Four sizes of clear silicone butt plugs, colored anal beads, her pink rabbit, the new purple vibrator, the tube of lube—cap open no less. She swallowed the enormous knot in her throat and blinked back the tears that were as ridiculous as they were warranted.

She glanced to the door and imagined what it looked like from their perspective. And...oh, fuck yeah. It was just as bad as she feared.

She slid her arms into silken sleeves and wrapped the robe around her like a shield. Why oh why had she thought she had the luxury of privacy? Stupid, stupid her!

Her gaze swept over the discarded bag, and she reached forward and scooped it off the floor. Quickly, in case her jackass roommates came barging in again, she threw everything back into it. Settling her feet on the floor, her right heel landed on something firm and wet. Fucking hell. She retrieved the red dildo and threw it in with the rest.

Jesus.

Oh, Jesus.

It was bad enough they'd caught her watching porn. It was absolutely horrifying they'd walked in on her masturbating. But on top of those nightmares, they'd seen her fucking herself with a ginormous red dildo. Oh, god! They'd seen her double fucking herself with it!

She allowed the bag to fall limply to the floor and cradled her head in her hands. She had a 50-50 shot, at best, of not regurgitating the margaritas.

Jack stood in the hall outside the door to the den, his mouth hanging open. His brain was stuck. Trapped on an involuntary playback loop. Still trying to decipher what the hell they'd just walked in on.

Just like the others, when he'd heard the man's voice, he'd reacted on instinct. All he could think was that someone was hurting Callie. In almost four years of living with them, she'd brought two guys home. One of whom they'd apparently scared away, much to her indignation. The other she'd dated for about six months. But the happy couple had spent most of their time at his place, saving the guys from hearing whatever it was she might've done with him when they were alone. Nothing in his experience with Callie had prepared him for the possibility of...holy fuck! Her masturbating to porn with a huge-ass fake cock? And was he tripping, or were those fucking butt plugs all over the coffee table?

He didn't know whether to freak out or jump for joy. Their girl was kinky!

Hands on his hips, Jack turned his head toward Noah, whose right hand covered his mouth while his left tugged back his soft curls. A blush showed through his light brown skin.

Noah dropped his hand from his face. "Was she—?"

"Sshh!" Lucas scolded.

"What?" Noah mouthed, hands out in question.

Jack rolled his eyes, but otherwise kept just as quiet.

"Let's give her some space," Lucas said, although the words ended on an upward lilt, belying his uncertainty in the suggestion.

"Nah, man," Jack whispered back. "She's flipping the fuck out in there. We gotta make this okay."

Noah bit his lip, weakly repressed humor crinkling the corners of his eyes. "Dude, I don't know how you make a woman feel better about her best friends walking in on her while she's masturbating to porn."

"Sshh!" Lucas punched Noah's bicep.

Noah rubbed his arm and scowled at Lucas. Jack sympathized—he'd been on the receiving end of Lucas's lethal punches a time or two himself.

Jack raised his eyebrows and shook his head. "I don't know, Noah. She's my fucking idol right now."

The guys traded glances. The atmosphere in the hallway electrified.

Lucas swallowed and collapsed against the wall. After a moment his gaze cut to Noah. Then he groaned and hung his head. "That was the hottest fucking thing I've ever seen in my life," he murmured.

Jack stepped toward Lucas. He beckoned Noah closer, bringing the three of them into a huddle. "Did you see what she was watching?"

"It was a threesome." Noah rubbed his jaw.

"Fuckin' A it was a threesome," Jack muttered. He looked at Lucas. "She was getting off to being with multiple guys."

"Would you keep it down?" Lucas bit out. "Oh Christ." He scrubbed his face with both hands. "She fucking was."

"Where the hell is that head of yours going, man?" Noah asked.

Jack stared back with a raised eyebrow, a plan taking shape in his mind, and waited.

Noah's gaze narrowed at Jack. "No. Are you serious?"

Jack nodded and smiled. "This. Is. It. This is three years of fucking desire served up on a silver platter. You two know you've wanted her." Jack pointed at the closed door behind him. "And apparently she's been wanting us, too. Or, at least, the idea turns her on."

"Jack, her watching that doesn't mean she wants *us*," Noah offered.

"Oh, come on," Jack said. "Callie is the total package, and yet it's been two years since she's dated anybody. She turns down other invitations to hang with us." He looked at Noah. "She cuddles with you on the couch watching movies and reads the Sunday paper in your bed. And she helped you plan your grandmother's funeral." He peered up at Lucas. "Whenever she has anything important she needs a date for, she asks you. She's taken you home for Christmas twice. When she needs advice, she goes to you before anybody. And you're the only one of us she's actually kissed for real." As for himself, Jack thought, the constant flirting and sexual innuendo between them, joking though it seemed, was often hot enough to drive him into the shower to jerk off.

Noah's whispered voice sounded serious. "If she even agreed to it, could you handle that, Lucas? Would us all being with her be okay with you?"

Lucas's face was blank for long moments as he stared at the floor.

"Fuck." He groaned then met both of their gazes. "I'd give that girl absolutely anything she ever wanted."

The three traded resolved expressions and nods and Jack said, "Okay. Let me handle this." Lucas and Noah opened their mouths, protest obvious in their dark gazes, but Jack cut them off with a hand to each of their chests. "Trust me."

Lucas shook his head, but finally nodded. Noah threw Jack a practiced glare that meant *don't fuck this up.*

Jack turned and knocked on the door.

CHAPTER FOUR

"Callie?"

No answer.

Jack knocked again. "Callie, I'm coming in. Okay?"

Still no answer.

Jack glanced back at Noah and Lucas. Luke nodded. Jack twisted the knob. He pushed the door slowly, giving her full warning this time as he peeked around the edge of the frame and found Callie wrapped in her pink robe with her face buried in her hands.

Jack closed the door behind him and walked into the room. With difficulty, he ignored the bag sitting by her left foot, but the protruding red dildo, like an arrow pointing and saying *look at me, look at me*, made that a little difficult. Finally, he dragged his gaze away and knelt in front of her.

Settling his knees on either side of Callie's feet, he scooted as close to her as he could. He smoothed his hands over her shoulders. Some part of him thought he should try to reassure her that what she'd been doing was perfectly natural, that it was just *them*, after all, and they loved her no matter what. But another part of him, a bigger part, argued that was the wrong way to go. Instinct told him if he tried to reason with her, it would add to her embarrassment rather than ease it. He debated for a moment, then kissed the crown of her head. Her pale honey hair skimmed like silk over his lips and smelled flowery and feminine.

Jack shifted to his left, allowing his lips to easily reach her ear. He pressed another chaste kiss there. "Callie? Come on." He stroked her shivering back. "Okay. How 'bout this? I'll talk. You listen."

She nodded, face still hidden.

He smiled. "'Atta girl. Okay. I won't lie to you. What I saw when I walked in here"—she stiffened under his touch—"was the hottest fucking thing I've ever seen."

"Jack," she groaned.

"No, you're just listening, remember? And I am telling the god's honest truth. Me and Noah and Lucas—especially Lucas, Callie—we're all a little in love with you, baby girl. And damn, seeing you like that, and knowing you were pleasing yourself to the idea of multiple guys? We're a bit insane right now, because we've all fantasized about you. God, have we." Jack swallowed thickly against her ear.

Callie turned her head so one eye peeked out through strands of blonde.

"So, we're offering." He grinned and kissed her temple. "I promise you nothing will change if we do, or if we don't. Because the three of us, we're yours for life. In whatever way you want us."

Callie knew the knock on the door would come. The only question was which of the three of them would be the one to walk through it. She'd braced herself when Jack knelt in front of her, braced herself against the awkward apology sure to come, against the friendly ribbing she deserved. She had no idea how she would ever be able to face these guys again.

But the words he said were not what she expected. The invitation he laid out for her—the invitation to *be* with them, to act out this fantasy for real *with them*—was completely outside anything she imagined possible.

She sat for a long moment, still mostly curled into herself. Her gaze lit on the rough bobbing of Jack's Adam's apple as he swallowed. His apparent case of nerves eased hers. A little. Soft, sandy-colored strands brushed against her forehead. Her nose filled with the scent of him, all night air and masculinity.

Callie took a deep breath, her body remembering her unfulfilled arousal even as her brain struggled to keep up. "What are you saying, Jack?" she whispered, buying herself time to think and needing him to spell it out.

One hand stroked her back while the other combed her hair off the side of her face. "I'm saying"—he nibbled at her ear, but this time his lips lingered, his warm exhalation caressing her skin—"that the three of us want to bring that fantasy to life for you. If you want."

Every nerve ending tingled with the promise of what he offered. Her heart rose from where it had plummeted into her gut and hammered against her chest. Images of the three of them kissing her, fucking her, swamped her brain. Blood roared through her ears. "Are you teasing me?"

"Look at me," he said, sliding his large hand under her cheek.

The commanding press of his skin on hers skittered electrical charges down her neck to her breasts. Her nipples hardened. She acquiesced and sat up just enough to face one of her three dearest friends.

"We want to do this for you." He quirked the sexiest of crooked smiles and shrugged with one shoulder. "You know we'd be good together."

She didn't know whether his "we" meant her and him or the four of them. An encouraging voice in her mind said both interpretations were true.

He cupped her neck, his grasp comforting and reassuring, and brushed his lips against her right cheekbone. Her right eye. Her forehead. Tilting his head to the other side, he repeated the action against her left eye, the apple of her left cheek. She gasped when his last kiss fell on that tender, hollow spot just below her ear.

"What do you want, Callie? Whatever you want, we want. Always."

His words tickled against her skin. She sucked in a breath. The warmth of his touch on her skin. The need in his voice. The invitation in his words. The passion promised by his lips.

The sexual fire within, which had gone from ice cold after the surprise of their interruption to low-burning embers when he'd laid out his proposal, now rekindled. Her body roared back to life with an enthusiastic affirmative, but her thoughts whirled with all the reasons this was ludicrous.

It was her mind that spoke: "I want to say 'yes', but I'm...scared."

His hand skimmed down her neck to her shoulder and squeezed. He pulled back and met her gaze. "You never have to be scared of us. You'd control the whole thing. Tell us what you want, what you don't want. This would be about you."

Oh, my god. How could she resist? But could she really go through with it?

Fantasizing was one thing, but this was the real deal.

She chewed on her bottom lip and stared into her lap, needing some relief from the intensity of Jack's gaze. Did she *want* to do it? Well, honestly, hell yes, she did. Would she regret it? She dragged her focus back to Jack, whose enthusiasm brought out the boyishness in his ruggedly handsome face framed by all those golden layers. She gave him a half smile and released an excited, shuddering breath. Whatever happened, they'd come out the other end of it just fine.

Come on, Callie, a small voice whispered from deep in her psyche.

"Oh, goddamnit," she muttered. "What the fuck."

Callie fell forward and found Jack's lips with her own. She groaned at the feeling of his mouth moving against hers. When he grunted his approval and wrapped his strong arms around her, Callie was done for. How many times had she wondered what this would be like?

Her hands fisted in his hair. God, it was thick and soft, and the harder she gripped it, the more eagerly his mouth claimed hers, the more aggressively his tongue explored her. The taste and scent of male spice inebriated her. The room spun. She sucked his tongue, pressing in, wanting to crawl into the moment.

She tried to move closer, but his hips and thighs trapped her calves together in front of her. Whimpering, she pulled his hair and swallowed his throaty groan. Jack rocked his hips forward, sliding the thick ridge of his cock between the crease in her joined knees. The sound and sensation brought to mind the thrill she'd imagined at the idea of being able to handle her guys. Jack's obvious arousal shoved away the last niggling bit of doubt.

"Christ." Jack leaned away, breathing hard.

His eyes were the deepest green Callie had ever seen.

He dragged his thumb along her bottom lip. "Your mouth is heaven," he ground out. He cupped her jaw. "But not here. We're doing this right." He rose and held out his hand.

Warmth bloomed in Callie's chest. With his words and gesture, he was already keeping his promise to make this about her, make this good for her. She slid her small hand into his big one and let him help her to her feet. Her gaze skittered between him and the door. As Lucas was the one who possessed the greatest share of her heart, Callie was most nervous to learn his reaction. But if this was the only way she'd ever have him, there was no way in hell she could turn it down. Adrenaline ripped through her, made her shiver.

"Remember," he said with a finger tilting her chin up. "It's what you want and no more."

Her body surged with the need to let pure, animal instinct take over. To shut down thinking and simply *feel*. She gave herself permission to do just that. "I'm all in, Jack."

His proud smile, falling across her like a physical touch, released butterflies in her stomach. He tugged her arm and ushered her forward.

But Callie wasn't going to be led into this. The only way she could triumph over her nervousness and embarrassment was to take charge. She patted Jack's corded bicep and stepped past him into the hall.

Noah's and Luke's heads whipped up at the sound of her footsteps. They stood, leaning against the wall, arms crossed over their broad chests. Damn, they were gorgeous men. And so different. Dark and sexy Noah, so sweet but a little shy. Lucas, god, Lucas. The quintessential rugged man. Tall, athletic, with a few small scars around his left eye that always cut an edge into his expression. A study in contrasts—tough *and* vulnerable, hard-ass *and* gentle.

Seeing them released whatever unease lingered. These were her men, her best friends. She walked right up between them, cupped both their faces and stroked their jaws. At her touch, they relaxed. The sense that she affected them so easily filled her with power.

Keeping a hold of Lucas with a tight fist in his shirt, she grasped Noah's neck and guided him to her. Their lips met in soft, dragging pulls that resonated down her body and settled in her curling toes. Noah threaded his right arm behind her and hugged her as he gave back every bit of the quiet intensity she unleashed on him.

Callie leaned back and gave him a small smile. He ducked his head a bit but maintained her gaze and returned her grin. Feeling confident about Noah's reaction, Callie backed away, but worked her left hand into his. Taking a deep breath to calm her racing heartbeat, she stepped up to Lucas and pushed herself onto tiptoes.

At twenty-seven, Lucas had been to war. Lost close friends. Witnessed unimaginable suffering and selfless heroism. But somehow, as Callie pressed her softness against him and explored his mouth, his whole life boiled down to this moment. The past three years, his whole goddamned future. They met right here.

Lucas hummed as he gave in to passion. He embraced her, crushed her against him. He would never get enough of her feminine curves. As their tongues twisted and tangled, he devoured her sweet taste. Christ, he couldn't get close enough, deep enough. He gripped her harder, lifted her off her feet. The moan she let loose was the most satisfied sound he'd ever heard, and pleasing her became his total mission in life—like it wasn't already. She stroked his hair, knowing how comforting he found that sensation, and his heart expanded and warmed at the thought she wanted to please him, too.

Lucas's mind screamed caution. This was the woman he adored, one of his best friends in the world. How many years had he ached for her? Yet, he'd held back, not wanting to saddle her with his anger, the night terrors, and headaches that lingered from the injury that had left him partially deaf. She was young—six years younger than him— and just starting out in the world. She didn't need his drama.

She sucked his tongue into her heat, dragging a low groan from him. God, he wanted this chance, this memory. As he dove back into the kiss, he gave himself temporary permission to get the fuck out of his head for just one night. To just feel. As soon as he did, his dick immediately hardened against her stomach. He groaned again when she writhed against his cock.

Callie unleashed an excited keening into Lucas's mouth, and his eyes flew open. Jack pressed his body against her back.

Lucas actually growled. *Mine, damn it!* Callie broke free but stroked his hair, massaged his neck.

Jack's husky voice came from behind her. "Why don't we take this upstairs? To *your* room, Luke."

Lucas interpreted the suggestion as a peace offering. And in less than a dozen words, Jack had just orchestrated what Lucas had been too damn scared to try to make happen—Callie in his bed. Lucas cut his gaze from Jack's chill-the-fuck-out expression to Callie. She smiled. He looked back to Jack and gave a small nod that said, *yeah, okay, chilling out over here*, and then voiced, "Yeah."

They moved as a unit. Callie danced from man to man as they stumbled down the hallway and up the stairs. She was always in someone's arms. Always touching and kissing. But still, no matter who was receiving the bulk of her attention at any given moment, she kept some connection with Lucas—holding his hand, rubbing up against him, fisting his shirt.

Their clumsy, handsy, lust-drunk trip to Lucas's room might've taken seconds or long minutes. It was impossible to tell. Time, space, the very laws and properties of physics seemed completely inapplicable to Lucas as he gave in to the pure pleasure of taking what he wanted, of getting what he needed.

Lucas flipped on a lamp as they stumbled into his room where his king-sized, iron-framed bed dominated the space. That is, right up until Callie climbed onto it, crawled to the center of the huge mattress, and settled into a kneeling position on the charcoal gray comforter. Dropping her gaze, she untied her robe. The thin pink fabric parted, baring her to their gazes from the graceful arch of her collarbone to the blonde curls of her pussy. Her eyes lifted and found Lucas's stare.

"Please," was all she said before all three men were in motion.

CHAPTER FIVE

Lucas was the first man on the bed. One thing he would never stand for was Callie Davis begging. Not when he was only too happy to give.

His gaze held hers, and she smiled as he pulled her into his arms. Their kiss was urgent, devouring. Lucas swallowed each of Callie's small whimpers and sounds, feeding his soul.

Her small, soft hands settled on his waist and tugged at his shirt. He sucked in a breath as Callie removed it, their mouths separating only long enough to pass the cotton over his head. Then he was right back, wanting everything he could have of her.

Callie explored his upper body. She massaged his shoulders. Traced the shrapnel and surgical scars the explosion had left all down the side of his ribs.

Scraped short fingernails over his erect nipples, tangled her fingers in the trail of hair leading down past his belly button.

Lucas pulled away from her lips and dropped his attention to her throat. Whenever she wore her hair up, his gaze always lingered on the long column of her beautiful neck. He thought of that now as he licked and nipped and sucked from her jaw line to her collarbone.

He pushed at the silk on her shoulder just enough to extend his exploration.

Her hand stroked his hair, held him to her. "Come closer," she whispered.

Lucas looked up as Callie beckoned Jack and Noah to join in. He hadn't even felt them get on the bed he'd been so into Callie.

Her gaze returned to his. "You can take it off." She shrugged at the robe hanging around her biceps and smiled at him.

Skimming his palms down her neck and over her shoulders, Lucas caught the fabric on her arms. He pushed until it slid off and puddled behind her. He totally understood the low moans of appreciation the others offered. Jack tossed the silk to the floor.

Swallowing hard, Lucas admired the woman before him. Her breasts were full and capped with pink, pebbled nipples. Her waist curved in before flaring out again at her hips. Her skin was tanned and soft as satin.

"Beautiful, Callie," he whispered.

Callie savored the gruff intensity of Lucas's voice. She kissed him one last time, then with his hand still in hers, she turned to Jack. She needed a break from the electricity ricocheting between her and Luke. It stole her breath, gripped her heart, and unleashed a torrent of emotion.

Jack's lips provided the perfect distraction. God, he was just as playful in bed as he was in every other part of his life. He attacked and withdrew, retreating whenever she tried to capture his tongue so she had to lean toward him to pursue. She only kept her balance by bracing one hand on his shoulder. He chuckled. Pure Jack.

Three pairs of hands teased and explored her body. Jack caressed the underside of her breasts. Noah stroked her back. Lucas's fingers walked down over her hip to her thigh. She gasped and writhed, wanting every bit of the contact. Each masculine touch spiked her arousal, readied her between her thighs. Jack grasped her face and held her to him for another searing kiss.

Once he freed her, she was a little dazed. She swayed and found Noah behind her, massaging her back and pressing sweet butterfly kisses across her shoulder blades. She reached back, tugged at his clothes. "Shirts off, both of you."

"Yes, ma'am," Jack replied. His Tee hit the floor the very next instant. So did Noah's. Damn. Broad, muscular chests and hot, male flesh surrounded her. She swallowed as her gaze raked over each of the men. They were all hers for the taking. At least for tonight. And she was damn sure going to make the most of it.

Heaving a deep breath, she drew her stare from the men's bodies and crossed her arms over her breasts. "Now," she said. She winked at Lucas and nailed Jack with a stern gaze. "You said I could have whatever I wanted, right?"

He grinned and nodded.

She waggled her finger between Jack and Noah. "Then I expect to see you two enjoying one another, too."

All three men went still.

She giggled at the flummoxed expression on Jack's face. It was nearly impossible to embarrass him or catch him off guard. She grabbed Noah's hand and pulled him closer.

"What do you think *started* all this anyway? I wasn't so obsessed with this particular fantasy until I saw the two of you together last weekend."

The boys traded glances, mouths gaping, eyes guarded.

"Next time, shut your door. Otherwise, I am so gonna watch that shit."

At her words, Jack's expression grew amused and his cheeks flushed.

Callie looked at Lucas. "Do you mind?"

He shook his head. "Whatever you want." He met Jack's gaze then Noah's. "I don't mind."

She pecked Lucas's cheek. She knew he'd be cool about them. "So, it's settled."

"Thank fuck," Noah muttered. His curse surprised her almost as much as the desperation with which he clutched Jack and planted an aggressive kiss on his open mouth.

Holy mother of kissing men! Callie turned so she could see them better and leaned back against Lucas's huge, hard chest. His warm fingers skimmed up her stomach and cupped her full breasts.

"Watching them turns you on?" he murmured against her ear.

The guys were so forceful with each other, and now that they didn't have to hide themselves, their passion burst uncontrollably from them. Masculine hands tugged hair. Bare, muscled chests pressed and rubbed. Erections ground together through denim.

"Yeah," she rasped.

"How about this?" Lucas asked and thrust himself against her bottom as his fingers plucked at her nipples.

She whimpered. "Yes."

"What else?"

"I want to see them naked," she whispered.

"Say it louder."

Callie swallowed. God, his commanding tone was sexy as hell. "I want to see them naked."

"You heard her," Lucas called out.

Without breaking their kiss, both men worked at the other's waistband in a rush to unbutton and unzip. Together, they tugged the denim roughly downward, off.

"Oh, shit," she mumbled as Lucas's hands disappeared from her breasts and fumbled behind her with his own pants. Only underwear separated her rear from his considerable bulge. She moaned at the sight of Jack's bare cock springing free against the other man's tight black boxers, the dark color of the fabric showing off the warm tones of Noah's mocha skin. Noah's own erection strained against the cotton. The evidence of her friends' arousal drew a low groan from her throat.

Jack tilted his head toward her. Noah took advantage of the movement and nipped and sucked at his neck. Jack licked his lips, his green eyes blazing. "What now, Callie-girl?"

"Touch each other."

"Already doing that." He flashed a cocky grin and stroked Noah's flexed bicep.

"Where, baby?" Lucas nibbled the shell of her ear. His hands rubbed down her ribs and gripped her hips. He thrust forward, letting his cock graze her bare ass.

She could do this. She met Jack's half-lidded gaze and pressed back against Lucas. "Strip him and stroke his cock."

Noah flashed her a smile. "Aw, yeah."

Jack wasted no time, removing those sexy underwear and grasping Noah's thick dick. Noah's smile dropped off his face, and his mouth shifted into a silent O. Jack pumped slow and soft at first, his whole fist gripping Noah's impressive girth, then he jerked him harder until Noah panted and grunted.

Callie and Lucas writhed together in a languid, torturous pace. While she drank in every detail of the men making out and masturbating one another, Lucas kissed and licked her ear, her neck, her shoulder, his hands constantly moving.

She turned her head and sought his lips. Their tongues twirled and danced, stealing her breath. Her pulse hammered under her skin. "You strip, too," she said between kisses.

He smiled and obeyed. When he slid his cock against the crease in her rear, the juices of her arousal coated her pussy. Every nerve ending in her body seemed connected to her clit. Callie shook with lust.

"Come closer, guys," she whispered, her form still pressed tightly to Lucas, his dick nestled between her ass cheeks.

They did as she asked. Jack crawled on all fours, the big tribal tattoo on his shoulder rolling with each movement. He grinned up at her right before his mouth captured a nipple. The sucking sensation speared straight down to her core.

She cried out. Her head fell back on Lucas's shoulder. She clutched hard at his hip with one hand and tugged at Jack's hair with the other. "More, Jack!" she gasped. The things that man could do with his mouth!

Jack let loose a strangled grunt, his breath hot on her breast. Callie's gaze trailed down Jack's magnificent body. She gawked at the image before her. Noah laid prone, his thick cock twitching, his head and shoulders disappearing under Jack's lower abdomen. Jesus! He was sucking Jack's cock.

"Oh, my god," she mumbled. "How does that feel, Jack?"

"Insane."

Lucas murmured in her ear. "I imagine it's a lot like this." He spun Callie around and, in one smooth move, laid her on her back. Her head landed on Noah's muscled thigh. Lucas climbed over her and without any preamble laved her wet folds.

Callie screamed. "Luke!" And she'd thought Jack was good with his tongue.

"God, you taste fantastic." He growled as he continued lapping at her wetness.

He licked tight circles over her clit until her thighs quivered. Only then did he suck her swollen nub into his mouth. The intensity of the strokes left her breathless. As her world spun and narrowed, becoming tighter and tighter, she arched her hips into his mouth, begging with her body for him to fill her aching need. He didn't tease. His probing tongue entered her, explored her. She cried out and caressed his hair. The delicious torment went on and on as Lucas pleasured her and drove her wonderfully mad.

Jack was close enough to reach her, and he took full advantage, once again teasing her sensitive nipples with his skilled mouth until Callie thought she might pass out.

Instead, she cursed and writhed, her body a live wire. She couldn't stay still. She turned her head and found Noah's thick cock twitching before her. Her hand wrapped around it before she'd even thought to do so. His dick was wider than anyone else's she'd ever been with. She licked his length, making him wet, and stroked his slick rod.

"Think he likes that," Jack panted against her sensitive breast.

Noah's groans rang out from where his face was buried in Jack's thrusting groin. Jack's mouth sucked harder as Noah devoured him.

"Jack," Callie panted. "Oh god, Lucas. Don't stop." She swallowed. "Jack, suck Noah, too."

He smiled up at her with shiny, swollen lips. "You'd like that, hmm?"

"Yes," she hissed. Enraptured, she watched Jack's mouth swallow Noah's shaft in one hungry motion until his chin touched her hand where she still held Noah's thick, hard length. "Oh, god." She pressed her thighs against Lucas's head, anchoring his attention between her legs. "Oh, god. I'm gonna come. Oh, god!"

A searing heat barreled through her veins. The electric tension congregated in her wet center then erupted outward. She screamed. Her whole body arched under Lucas's relentless attention. Her toes curled and dug into the comforter. Her cunt contracted again and again.

"Fucking phenomenal," Jack whispered, then plunged right back down on Noah's leaking rod.

In the next moment, a heavy weight covered her, warming and thrilling her. Lucas's mouth landed on hers, his tongue begging for entrance. Callie was only too happy to grant access. She tasted herself on him and moaned at the decadence of its flavor and scent.

"What now, Callie?" he asked, a pleading tone straining his voice.

The need in his words chased her satiation away. Her pussy ached to be filled. Her head spun in wonder that she could finally have Lucas. "Fuck me," she answered

Lucas's hazel eyes darkened. His brow furrowed.

Callie frowned and stroked his soft brown hair. "What is it?"

He stared at her for a long moment. She could almost see the thoughts whirling behind his intense gaze. Finally, he leaned down and whispered for her alone to hear. "I will *never* just fuck you. Even when I take you hard and fast—and I will—it won't ever be just fucking."

Callie sucked in a breath. There was only one other thing it could be then, right? One other thing you could call it? Her eyes stung with unexpected emotion. She tilted her face toward him and turned his head so she could whisper in his good ear. "It will never be just fucking for me, either."

He groaned, a sound full of satisfaction, and kissed her like he might never have another chance.

All of a sudden, his warm weight disappeared. She missed the encompassing feel of him immediately. Her gaze followed him as he rolled off the bed and picked up his jeans from the floor. He grinned at her while he fished his wallet from a back pocket. God, his body was phenomenal, all carved muscle, his unit insignia inked on one thick bicep. Scars marked his rib cage, a badge of honor and bravery she found utterly sexy. She hummed her approval.

A deep grunt captured her attention, and she dragged her attention to Jack and Noah. They were still sucking each other off, but were now lying on their sides in a sixty-nine position. Jack had his arms wrapped around Noah's hips, his face buried in Noah's dark curls, his throat clearly filled with his lover's massive cock. She salivated as she watched, then needing to touch, Callie reached out and grasped Noah's ass. She squeezed and massaged his rear. He cried out and bucked against Jack. Becoming more brazen by his response, she swiped both thumbs between his cheeks and grazed his entrance.

"Fuck. *Fuck*, coming," he groaned.

Callie's eyes met Jack's as he swallowed the other man's cum. When he released Noah, he wiped the corner of his mouth and winked at Callie. She stretched over Noah and plunged her tongue into Jack's mouth. Noah's musky release infused Jack's natural taste. Her head spun as sensation upon new sensation whirled through her body.

Two strong, warm hands grabbed and guided Callie across the mattress.

She gasped at the manhandling and chuckled at the wicked grin on Lucas's face. His long, thick cock jutted toward her, a tiny drop of pre-cum clinging to its pink head. His balls were high and tight. She watched him sheathe himself in latex, thrilling anticipation fluttering in her stomach and lighting up her veins.

Licking her lips, hungry for more of what he had to give, she held her arms open to him.

He climbed up her body, kissing, claiming, and slid his dick against her drenched cunt. "Baby, what do you want?"

CHAPTER SIX

"I need you in me, Luke. Please? I'm aching for you."

Callie's breathless voice fell over him like a caress. "Christ," he rasped. "I know just what you mean."

Lucas propped himself on one elbow and reached between them. Taking his dick in hand, he dragged the tip back and forth over her clit. He couldn't believe this was happening. Couldn't believe he was about to be *inside* his Callie. *His* Callie. No matter what else happened here tonight, he wasn't going to go without saying what needed to be said.

"I need you *now.*" She lifted her hips in search of his cock.

He smiled at the hint of a whine in her tone and full-out grinned as he caught sight of the pouty lower lip that confirmed her impatience.

"You have me." He positioned himself at her opening and thrust. He filled her inch by delicious inch. Damn, she was tight. Her pussy gripped him like a velvet fist, pulling, squeezing, teasing. Her sweet juices flowed, easing the way, helping her body adjust to what he knew was a considerable invasion. Balls-deep inside her, he bit out a strained, "Oh, fuck."

He was making love to Callie Davis.

Wanting to watch as he took her, Lucas braced himself above her, his fists planted into the bed on either side of her rib cage. Small sighs and breathy grunts spilled from her glossy pink lips each time his body rocked into hers. Her breasts bounced in tandem with the rhythm he set, slow and seductive to start. Glancing down, he watched as his glistening dick penetrated and withdrew from her soft folds.

"Oh, my god, that's hot," she said.

Lucas's attention snapped back to Callie's radiant face. Propped up on one elbow, she licked her lips, her gaze locked on the advance and retreat of his wet cock.

He nodded. "Looks incredible, but feels fucking unbelievable. You are perfection, Callie."

She fell back against the bed and dug her nails into his sides. "Oh, harder, Luke."

Whatever you wish. Threading one hand under her left knee opened her legs farther. She groaned at the change in position and arched her back. He groaned at the eroticism of the image. His pelvis slapped against hers. His shaft drove to her very depths. He held her gaze as he claimed her—damn if her eyes weren't heaven in a stare. Her slick walls milked him, called him home. His powerful thrusts rocked them closer and closer to the headboard. But there was no stopping, no holding back.

Callie was on fire. Lucas's cock was incredible. He filled and stroked her as no one ever had before. She'd seen him dance, had gone out with the guys many times to the clubs around town, and she'd often imagined the way he worked his hips on the dance floor would translate into some goddamned good sex. And fuck, it was so true. He swiveled his hips then hammered. Rolled his hips so they ground against her clit and filled her with long, deep strokes. He kept her guessing, kept her right on the edge. She was a rope pulled taut and fraying at the center.

And damn, he was so attentive—observing, watching, learning what pleased her body. He repeated the motions that elicited the most pleasurable sounds from her. He touched and kissed and moved against her in search of those secret spots on her body that set her ablaze. And damn, he found them, again and again. He positioned himself to ensure his dick teased the most sensitive areas inside her. The base of his cock stimulated her until she whimpered nonstop.

But it was his little murmured terms of endearment, the *gratitude* that dripped from his words, the adoration that burned in his eyes—these were the things that elevated the physical act from simply great sex to a life-changing encounter.

Lucas picked up the pace as Jack slipped in behind Callie's head to keep her from being slammed into the headboard. Leveraging his hands under her arms, Jack hiked her shoulders up into his lap. Completely focused on Lucas, she gasped at the unexpected movement. Half-dazed, she looked up into Jack's smiling face.

"Relax," he whispered. Then he reached around and grasped her breasts, squeezing them together and rolling her nipples between his fingers.

She groaned and met Jack's lust-drunk gaze. "Noah?"

"No worries. He'll be right back. Just feel, baby girl."

Callie knew what she wanted to feel. Jack's hard length pressed against her neck. She shifted to her right and turned her head, allowing Jack's cock to jut forward. She leaned in until she could lick and mouth the side of it.

"Fuck, Callie, you don't have to—"

"Relax." She grinned before licking again.

She shifted so she could reach him better. She couldn't move a lot in this position, particularly with how Lucas pounded into her, but her mouth salivated in want of Jack's dick. She engulfed his smooth tip with her ovaled lips. Her nose filled with the scent of Jack's musk. She smiled around the girth of his cock when his head banged against the headboard.

Lucas shifted, and the angle was heaven. Callie groaned and looked up at him. "Again," she panted, still stroking Jack with her fist. Lucas's gaze flashed and narrowed, and he obeyed. For a long moment, Callie's eyelids sagged shut in response to the maddening sensation. Finally, she returned to Jack and sucked him hard and deep. Strangled grunts erupted from her as Jack filled her mouth and Lucas owned her pussy.

Lucas released her leg and lowered himself onto his elbows. He nipped at Callie's exposed neck and rolled his pelvis against the nerves at the top of her pussy.

Callie's body detonated. A high-pitched keening ripped from her throat. She released Jack from her ministrations. Her head arched backward into his thigh as her entire body flexed. Lucas slowed his strokes, but the way he tilted his hips lengthened and intensified her orgasm, because the new position stimulated her G-spot until tears spilled from the corners of her eyes.

Finally, Callie could focus again. Lucas was still hard inside her. Panting, she licked her lips and smiled at him.

"Beautiful," he whispered.

Lucas's seductive gaze was penetrating, laser-focused. In fact, now that she had more than two functioning brain cells again, she noticed all three men were staring at her. Jack looked down at her from behind, and Noah watched from the edge of the bed.

She held her arm out to Noah.

He managed to grin and blush at the same time. "Why don't you get on top of Lucas?"

Damn, but his cuteness made him hot.

Breathing hard, Callie nodded. She rose and claimed Luke's mouth, connecting them through sucking lips and twirling tongues. As they kissed, she slowly sat them up. Lucas's grip held the condom in place over his straining dick as he withdrew. Her body missed his full presence immediately, but she knew it was only temporary.

"Is this okay?" she asked.

He quirked a half smile. "You riding me? Yeah, more than okay."

She attacked the bottom of his rib cage with her fingers, finding his ticklish spot immediately.

He barked out a laugh and twisted away. Grinning, he manacled her wrists in his tight grip and pulled her in for another searing kiss before lying along the edge of the bed.

Callie pressed her lips against his flat stomach. He smelled of Ivory soap and her. She licked the ridges of his muscles, tasting the saltiness of his sweaty skin. Lucas groaned, his stomach clenching and unclenching. If his dick hadn't been sheathed, she'd have tasted him there, too. Next time. She could only hope.

Instead, she climbed up his body on all fours and straddled him, savoring the idea that in this position she'd get a perfect view of his face when he came.

"Take your time, baby," he whispered.

"I know," she said. "But I'm already missing the feeling of you inside me."

She reached between them, found Lucas's swollen cock, and slipped it back into her drenched channel. They both sighed. She rode him slowly. He pulled her down and wrapped his arms around her neck and shoulders. He sucked at her lips—first her bottom one, then her top. His pelvis took over their movements as his hard length rocked in and out of her pussy.

The other men's caresses and kisses fell onto her lower back, her hips, her ass. Three pairs of hands touched her, igniting a flame within her. She imagined how she looked, three men exploring and pleasuring her. She whimpered into Lucas's eager mouth.

Something cool pressed against her exposed anus—a finger slicked with lube. She squirmed in surprise.

"Sshh," Noah soothed.

He gently pushed through the ring of muscle at her opening, sinking deep. Callie gasped and rested her turned head on Lucas's broad shoulder so she could see who was teasing her rear.

Noah stood next to the bed. One of his hands stroked and separated her ass cheeks. The other slowly fingered the cleft. His face was a mask of desire— mouth open, eyes molten.

Her heart took off at a sprint, vibrated against Lucas's sternum. "Try more," she breathed.

Lucas's palms skimmed over her hair, down her spine. "Just relax for him. Just feel. We can go very slow." He nuzzled the sweet spot under her ear.

Jack's silky hair fell on her back along with a few gentle kisses from him. "He's right. What you want, how you want, remember?"

She nodded, her forehead resting on Luke's shoulder again, and moaned low in her throat when Noah added a second wet digit.

"Doing so good," Noah murmured as he pressed his fingers a little deeper.

"I can take more," she rasped, moving her hips experimentally with both Lucas and Noah inside her.

"I don't want to hurt you."

"You won't. I...well...I've done it with four fingers."

All three men reacted. Noah smiled, and his reawakened cock twitched. Jack groaned and muttered somewhere behind her. Lucas bit down on the soft tendon above her collar bone.

She squeaked. "Hey!" She turned and cocked a brow at Luke.

"Baby, you can't *say* shit like that right now. I am *in* you, and it's fucking fantastic. And I can feel *him* through you. And it's a little mind-blowing. I can't picture you—"

She grinned and devoured his words with a lingering kiss. A third finger entered her. She gasped into Lucas's mouth and wriggled her ass at the intrusion. Laying her head back onto Lucas's shoulder, she moaned, "Yes, yes." All of the guys' movements were slow, gentle, driving Callie insane with need. "Please, you guys. Move. I need you to move."

Lucas flexed his hips to guide his cock in and out of her slick pussy. Noah finger-fucked her ass, twisting his wrist from time to time to vary the sensation. Callie's body melted on top of Lucas as she gave in to the demands of the pleasure they provided.

"Oh, my god. So good, guys. So...mmm...I want more."

Cold fluid dripped against her crack. Noah gave her his fourth finger. She hummed, the stretching motion and sensation of fullness a little uncomfortable, but there was something about the mixture of pleasure and pain that heightened her arousal, lit every nerve ending.

A hand landed against her ass in a slap that was louder than it was hard.

She cried out in surprise. "Oh, fuck. Again."

"Like that?" Jack rasped. "Do you like being spanked while Luke and Noah fuck you?"

"Yes!"

Each blow vibrated around Noah's invasion. Soon, the initial discomfort morphed into a tormented pleasure that dismantled her into a million pieces. She strained as her whole being convulsed. Lucas's arms strapped her to his chest, and the extra fullness in her anus made every contraction shudder throughout her body. Luke grunted as her cunt milked him. Noah withdrew his fingers, and she screamed with the eruption of another mini-orgasm.

"Fuck, you are hot," Jack complimented. He stroked her back. "What do you want, Callie? And, remember, it's okay if the answer is nothing."

"No, no. I want...uh..."

"What, baby?" Lucas panted in her ear. "Don't be shy."

Still, her face heated. "I want to be fucked."

Lucas thrust upward into her. "Mission accomplished." His cocky grin challenged her.

She raised an eyebrow. "Okay, then. I want to be double fucked."

Luke sucked in a breath. "Jesus."

Callie bit her bottom lip as she grinned at the strain on his face. But she also needed to know how he felt about what she wanted. She leaned down and in a hushed tone said to him, "I don't have to do this. I mean, if it's not...if it would make you feel—"

He kissed her, cutting off her words, whispering back, "Fuck, Callie, all I want is to make your dreams come true. But, I..." A growl rumbled deep in his throat. A shadow passed over his expression for just a moment before his eyes darkened with resolve. One hand tightened in her hair, pulled just a little. "Your pussy's mine, though. Just as long as your pussy's only mine."

Callie's cunt coated Lucas's cock inside her at the possessiveness of his words. "Yes. Yours."

"Say it again," he bit out, his words fanning her ear hotly.

"My pussy is only yours."

He bit and licked the shell of her ear. "Then what do you want?"

She looked over her shoulder at Jack and Noah. She reached out a hand to Noah and pulled him so she could see him better. "I don't want to hurt your feelings. Do you mind if Jack—"

He was already shaking his head. "Course not—"

"No, wait, please. I want to explain." She glanced down at his impressive girth. "It's just that"—she shrugged—"you're, um, well, *huge*, Noah." Her face flushed. "And this is my first time."

He bent over and pecked her on the mouth. She grabbed his curls and deepened the kiss, sucking his tongue deep and rhythmically. He smiled against her lips. "I understand. And, thanks." Noah stepped back and winked.

Callie blushed harder and smiled.

The bed jiggled, and Jack's hard chest fell across her back. He nuzzled her cheek. "I'll be gentle, I swear. And all you have to do is say 'stop' or 'slow down', okay?"

"I'm not worried. I know you'd never hurt me, Jack. None of you would."

"That's right. And"—he playfully bit her shoulder blade—"you can work up to Noah. He feels fantastic, but I can tell ya from experience, that boy has one big dick."

Callie's laughter stole her breath, especially when she saw the pink tinting Noah's cheeks again. "Thank you," she mouthed over her shoulder to Jack. His playfulness released most of the tension that built as she anticipated both of them being inside her.

From the corner of her eye she saw Jack roll on a condom and apply lube. She groaned as his fingers probed her anus, adding more lubricant.

"Are you sure, Callie?"

"Now, Jack. Please."

Lucas tugged at her hair. She faced him. He captured her lips in a scorching kiss that distracted her as Jack pressed his cock inward.

Noah's warm palm cupped her breast, teased her hard nipple. "Just relax for him," he murmured. "Let him in. He's gonna make you feel so good, Callie."

She moaned nonstop. The head of Jack's cock penetrated her tight entry. He paused. Hands caressed her everywhere. He moved another inch, then another. Each time, he stopped and let her body adjust. Callie's head spun at the overload of sensation. The process was slow and frustrating, delicious and a little scary. But Jack's obvious care not to hurt her reduced her fear to almost nothing. He pushed in farther. Rested. Then again. His balls grazed her pussy.

She'd taken him all! She'd taken them both! "Mmm…oh my fuck!"

"Damn, Callie, you're doing so good," Jack rasped. "Are you okay?"

"God, yes. I am so full."

Lucas groaned. "The mouth you have on you, girl."

She half-laughed, half-whimpered at him.

Still letting her adjust, Jack eased out before pushing back in. Next time, he withdrew a little more, then gently sank deeper.

"Aw, fucking hell," came Jack's strained voice from behind her. "You're amazing, baby."

Callie moaned and let their touch, their words, their heat wash through her.

Double penetration was without a doubt a total-body experience. The fullness affected not just her pussy and ass, but her thighs, hips, and stomach. The walls of her cunt quivered as the men moved within her, as they rubbed against one another through the thin membrane. Jack's cock stroking her rear made every nerve ending tingle and flare. An erotic soundtrack filled the air—her constant moaning, Jack's stream of muttered expletives and encouragements, Lucas's guttural grunts, the bed shifting under them, their bodies slapping together. Callie rested her head on Luke's shoulder, and her gaze immediately tracked the source of yet another sound, a quicker rhythmic friction—Noah stroking his fat cock.

"Come here," Callie said to him. "Right here." She directed him in front of her face. "I've been dying for a cock in my mouth all night. I want to see if I can handle yours."

His cheeks flushed, but he nodded. "I've no doubt." He pressed his legs hard against the side of the mattress to align his cock with her.

Wow. He *was* enormous! She relaxed her jaw to accommodate him. The heavy weight of his dick on her tongue was phenomenal. His taste was all Noah, warm and spicy.

She released him and looked up through her eyelashes. "You move, Noah. It's a little hard for me..."

He squeezed his eyes shut and groaned. "Okay."

He petted her hair and fucked her face. Panting and whimpering, she opened wide for him as he guided his thick cock between her hungry lips over and over. Peering up at him, she savored the guileless pleasure that shaped his beautiful face.

Callie moaned around Noah's dick, her body rocking as Lucas and Jack fucked her. This was it. She was doing it. *They* were doing it. She was handling all three of her guys. And it was indescribable. Their pleasured sounds made her feel desirable. Their desperation made her feel beautiful. Their praise made her feel strong, powerful. She moaned louder, whimpered, gasped.

"Callie," Lucas rasped. "I can't—fuck! I'm coming!"

She pulled free of Noah and faced her lover—truth be told, her love. "Yes, baby. Come in me." She stroked his hair.

His eyes clenched and square jaw locked open. "Oh, fuck. Oh, fuck yes!"

God, Lucas was magnificent. Her chest filled with a sudden warm pressure.

Callie swallowed around a lump in her throat and forced herself to focus on their bodies. Inside her, his cock still pulsed. "I can feel you," she whispered.

He threaded his hands into her hair and claimed her with a possessive kiss. Finally, he slumped against the bed in a well-used heap. Her breathing erratic, she bit her lip and grinned at him.

A hand tucked Callie's hair behind her ear and grabbed her attention. She remembered Noah and turned back to him, mouth salivating, ready to receive him.

He groaned and penetrated her, his girth filling her completely.

Jack grasped Callie's hips and repositioned her up onto her knees, free of Noah and Lucas.

"Oh god, Jack," she gasped when he pumped her ass with a driving, fast rhythm, much harder than before.

"Too much?" he asked, his voice a raw scrape.

"No. Good." Her face to the side, she allowed Noah to quiet her again with his needy cock.

Only Noah's thick shaft kept her from screaming when Jack reached around and rubbed fast circles over her clit. A second hand added to the pleasure between her legs before brushing Jack's fingers away. Lucas. Her eyes flashed to his. He'd removed Jack's hand from touching her there. Her pussy clenched. She panted out, "Yours."

He nodded, his hazel eyes blazing.

She devoured Noah's cock again, but didn't forget Lucas's heated expression. God, the intensity of that look shot right through her and pooled in her cunt. Each thrust of Jack's dick in her ass shoved her closer and closer. She sucked at Noah's cock, flicking her tongue, swallowing around him. Damn. She couldn't restrain the constant moaning. The whole night had been so wild. Unbelievably, her body lurched toward the edge once more.

"Damn, Callie. Oh, damn. I'm—" Noah stepped back.

"Uhn-uhn," she chided as best she could around a mouthful of thick dick. Her arm shot out and grabbed his hip. She tugged him tightly to her.

His mouth fell open, and he grunted. "Oh...oh, here I come."

Noah's cum streamed into her mouth. She swallowed as fast as she could, but his cock took up so much room, and she was already short of breath from Jack's demanding pace. Some spilled out over her lip and ran down her chin.

Jack leaned over her, watching. "Oh, Christ, Callie, you can't wear his cum. Oh, fuck me. It's all yours, baby." One, two, three strokes, and Jack's cock pulsed in her tight ass. His hands gripped her waist roughly as his body jerked and spasmed.

Lucas's fingers zeroed in on her clit and swirled her juices in fast circles around it until she thought she'd lose her mind. Tugs and flicks at her swollen nub unleashed Callie's orgasm. She cried out, her weight sagging onto Luke's chest. This release felt no less fantastic for being softer, quieter. They'd wrung more pleasure out of her body than she'd ever known before.

Jack rested his forehead against her back as his body calmed. He kissed her shoulder and eased out of her.

She collapsed onto Lucas, fully contented, happy, and exhausted beyond belief. "You were perfect. All of you," she whispered, swallowed hard. "Being with you was a thousand times more amazing than I thought it would be."

"You were the perfect one," Jack murmured, squeezing her hand.

"Yeah, that's the God's honest truth." Noah's deep voice came to her as he walked around the bed to the other side.

Lucas's strong arms hugged her. The embrace was warm and comforting, but she longed for his words. He was the only one who hadn't said something in return. Her tired heart raced in fear.

Oh god, what if he wasn't okay with this after all?

CHAPTER SEVEN

Long minutes later, Callie was asleep, her body sprawled across Lucas. Her presence there was the only thing keeping his heart from exploding right out of his rib cage.

Lucas had always recognized his feelings for her. She'd had the guts and grace to dress down a war-hardened veteran just when he needed it. Her actions had created a place for him to belong among this foursome of best friends, had started healing the big chip of rage and grief carved out of his shoulder, and had helped him find a path to becoming a better man. Every moment since then suggested his soul had met its match.

But the fear of ruining—or, really, altering in any way negatively—what he already had with her had trapped him in a holding pattern.

Until tonight.

Now he'd had her body, received her tantalizing declaration that they were *not* just fucking. Now he'd seen her, so free and guileless, her face so full of wonder and ecstasy. He couldn't imagine not having her like this, couldn't imagine his life without her.

It wasn't just the sex. Lucas was an experienced man. He had standing invitations from several women whenever his needs demanded fulfillment. But being with Callie was different, even given tonight's circumstances. She engaged not just his libido, but his heart and his head. She gave more than she took—just the way she'd maintained physical contact with him the *entire* night despite the others requesting some of her love. Her every action told him she considered him more important, every soothing caress of her hand said she cared.

The question was how much? Did she feel for him even a little of what he felt for her?

Lucas was so mesmerized by Callie's warm weight on his body, by the silkiness of her hair falling across his ribs—by his thoughts—that when he finally bothered to pay attention, he found himself the only one still conscious. Jack had collapsed face-down in the middle of the bed, and Noah lay on the far side of Jack.

Lucas stretched his neck, trying hard not to jostle Callie. The LED on the alarm clock glowed 10:47 PM. He nearly chuckled. This was just about the time they would've gotten home if they'd actually gone to the baseball game. It was still early for him. He was something of a night owl. But his body was spent. Just the restraint it had taken to hold off his orgasm for her had exhausted him in the best possible way.

It wasn't too long before Lucas found himself giving in to sleep.

Lucas gasped awake. For a moment he was disoriented, a sensation quickly replaced by a flood of pleasure. He glanced down.

Callie straddled his knees, and with her breasts dangling teasingly against his thighs, sucked his cock deeply into her mouth.

"Callie. What are you doing to me? Don't stop," he said, his low voice gravelly.

She caressed his thighs in response. He was surprised at her relative silence. She'd revealed herself all night to be seductively vocal. But he also liked it, because if they could both restrain themselves, they just might manage to share this moment without the audience of Noah and Jack.

Though honestly, he was at peace with what they'd all shared. Callie had loved the sex, and it brought her to his bed, allowing them to have the most fantastic physical and emotional experience of his life.

She flicked her tongue all over him as she moved up and down. The suction she could generate was crazy. It certainly drove him insane to the point where he could no longer talk. His head dropped back against the pillow, jaw slack, mouth open, eyes clenched, as he called on every ounce of will to control his orgasm.

But then she took him deeper. His cockhead met her throat again and again. Combined with the wet heat and the sucking, it was more than he could take.

"Oh, Jesus, coming, baby," he rasped.

He erupted within her. She squeezed his hip and swallowed his streaming jets of semen. He bit down on his lip to keep himself silent. But even that nearly failed as she continued to lave his over-sensitized cock.

Panting, he whispered, "That was so nice, Callie. Get up here." He kissed her, plunging his tongue inside her sweet mouth to taste their flavors swirling together. "Thank you."

"Any time." She chuckled and waggled her eyebrows. "You woke me up, er, poking me in the stomach, so I couldn't resist returning the favor."

Flickering images of the dream he'd been having barreled back into his consciousness. Lucas grinned. "I'm glad you didn't. And I hope there's another time."

She settled into the crook of his arm. "Me, too."

He fell asleep with a smile on his lips, contented by the feeling he was right where he belonged.

"When are you going to fucking tell her?" Jack had been on him for ten minutes now, ever since they'd both awakened while Callie and Noah still slept.

"Jesus, Jack," he retorted quietly. "As soon as I can."

"Now. This morning. Why wait?"

Noah rubbed his face, obviously awakened by the constant back and forth between Lucas and Jack.

"Hey, babe," Jack greeted Noah.

Lucas watched the two men kiss as his friend's words whirled through his head. It was different seeing his best friends interact this way, but they were so damn close anyway, it fit. He totally got it.

"Hey. What's up?" Noah asked in a voice still full of sleep.

"Our man here needs a little ass kicking is all."

Noah turned his head and frowned. His golden eyes narrowed.

Lucas groaned and covered his eyes. They were going to double team him.

"Dammit, Lucas. Claim her already. I couldn't fucking stand it if she ended up with someone outside of this room. And the two of you were made for each other," Noah said in a rough voice.

Lucas dropped his hand at Noah's curse and glanced at the younger man. They all knew Noah only resorted to such language when he was riled up, which, given how laid back he was, wasn't often.

"That's the fucking truth," Jack agreed, leveling Lucas with a stare full of wisdom.

He heaved a deep breath. Lucas knew his friends were right, knew it soul-deep. But he needed a little peace to get his head straight.

Jack turned toward Noah and ran his hand through the other man's dark curls. The gesture was surprisingly intimate, and Lucas almost felt he was intruding. The guys' open affection unleashed a yearning in his gut.

"Hey, baby," Jack murmured. "How about we head down to my room and give Luke and Callie some space? There's a conversation I'd like to have with you, too."

Noah blushed. "Oh, yeah?"

Jack nodded and grinned. "Yeah."

They eased out of bed and stumbled bare-assed together across the room. Noah looked back and gave Lucas a stern nod before he shut the door.

Lucas sighed and shook his head.

On the one hand, he was thrilled to finally be alone with Callie in his bed. On the other, he had no one left to run interference. He glanced down...into Callie's completely awake and observing baby blues.

"Hey. Er, how long have you been awake?"

She stretched against him. "Um, since 'the two of you were made for each other,' I guess."

"Fuck." He scrubbed at his face. He knew what he needed to do, but had wanted a few moments to figure out what to say, to gather his wits about him. That was a little hard to do with Callie's silky blonde hair splayed over his skin and his morning wood trapped under the heat of her soft thigh.

"Why 'fuck'?" She slid off him and away, propped her head on one elbow.

He cursed himself inwardly. Her expression was wary with a hint of hurt. That wouldn't fucking do.

"It's just...shit. I'm no good at this." He shook his head, trying to clear his thoughts. He grabbed her hand and kissed her knuckles. The soft scent of her skin calmed him. "I'm...Callie...." He shifted up, mirroring her position, so he could look down into her eyes. "I'm completely fucking in love with you. Have been for years. And I'm terrified you don't feel the same way and that I'm hurting the incredible friendship we have by even saying these things. Fuck."

Her earnest, bright eyes searched his gaze. "I love all three of you."

His stomach plummeted. "Oh, shit. I knew it—"

Callie's fingers covered his mouth. "Please, just listen. I love all three of you. You're my best friends. But, Lucas—hey, look at me now." She held his face in her hands. "I am *in love* with you. I'm not sure I truly admitted it to myself until last night. But the minute you were inside me, baby, the most amazing sense of…I don't know—"

"I do. A sense of being home. Of being found. Of being filled to the fucking brim with life. That's how you made me feel."

"Yes." Her breath hitched.

"Aw, don't cry." Lucas swiped at the tear that leaked from the corner of her eye with his thumb. "I love you, Callie."

"I love you, too."

Lucas's heart swelled until it was difficult to breathe. But as soon as their lips met in their first kiss as a couple, his body eased at the fundamental *rightness* of their declarations. He gasped and pulled away.

"What is it?" she asked.

"I don't want to lose you."

She smiled. "I'm not going anywhere."

"No, I mean...you haven't said anything, so I figured....When are you moving to New York?"

Her expression froze then softened. "I was going to tell all of you at brunch this morning. Surprise you."

He nodded, schooling his expression to hide his anxiety.

Her face beamed under the halo of blonde hair. "I accepted the National Geographic job Friday afternoon. I start July first."

"What?" She was staying here, in D.C.? His heart thundered against his sternum.

"Like I said, I'm not going anywhere."

He kissed her until she moaned, then chuckled. He pulled away. His cheeks ached from the width of his smile. He didn't care. "Be with me, Callie. Be mine. Move in here"—he motioned around his room—"with me."

She gaped, but gifted him with a brilliant smile.

He could almost see her thoughts playing out across her face. He grinned. "Come on. Just say, 'what the f—'"

She hugged him, pressed her lips against his throat, then pulled back and stroked his hair. He leaned into her touch. "No. That doesn't apply here, Lucas. Because, I *choose* you. I'm not gonna say 'what the fuck,' because I don't feel I'm just throwing caution to the wind. This wouldn't be a whim. I've dreamed of this, of *you*, for years. Now you've made me feel safe and secure enough to make this decision, even as quick as it's happening. And we feel so right to me."

"God, Callie, me, too."

"So instead"—she kissed him again and smiled—"I just gotta say this...I love you, Lucas Branson, and I'm yours."

WANT MORE SEXY CONTEMPORARY ROMANCE BY LAURA KAYE?

CHECK OUT

Hearts in Darkness

Two strangers...

Makenna James thinks her day can't get any worse, until she finds herself stranded in a pitch-black elevator with a complete stranger. Distracted by a phone call, the pin-striped accountant catches only a glimpse of a dragon tattoo on his hand before the lights go out.

Four hours...

Caden Grayson is amused when a harried redhead dashes into his elevator fumbling her bags and cell phone. His amusement turns to panic when the power fails. Despite his piercings, tats, and vicious scar, he's terrified of the dark and confined spaces. Now, he's trapped in his own worst nightmare.

One pitch-black elevator...

To fight fear, they must reach out and open up. With no preconceived notions based on looks to hold them back, they discover just how much they have in common. In the warming darkness, attraction grows and sparks fly, but will they feel the same when the lights come back on?

Dare to Resist

*Trapped and tempted, this battle of wills rages all night long...*Kady Dresco and Colton Brooks click on a level that defies logic. There are only two problems. One, he's her older brother's irritating best friend, and two, they're bidding on the same military security services contract.

When the competition heats up,

Colton is torn between wanting to strangle Kady (and her annoying brilliance) and kissing her into *submission*. Which is a bad idea for a million reasons, because Kady's submission is exactly what he craves. Being trapped in a tiny motel room with the object of his darkest fantasies will require every ounce of his restraint.

Kady doesn't want his restraint, but Colton knows better. She deserves love, marriage, and a white picket fence— three things Colton can't give her. But her proximity and the memory of their steamy near-miss three years ago slowly destroys his resolve. And he's not sure how much longer he can keep his hands off...or his heart closed.

THE HARD INK SERIES
Five dishonored soldiers
Former Special Forces
One last mission
These are the men of Hard Ink...

Hard As It Gets (Hard Ink #1)

Tall, dark, and lethal...

Trouble just walked into Nicholas Rixey's tattoo parlor. Becca Merritt is warm, sexy, wholesome—pure temptation to a very jaded Nick. He's left his military life behind to become co-owner of Hard Ink Tattoo, but Becca is his ex-commander's daughter. Loyalty won't let him turn her away. Lust has plenty to do with it too.

With her brother presumed kidnapped, Becca needs Nick. She just wasn't expecting to want him so much. As their investigation turns into all-out war with an organized crime ring, only Nick can protect her. And only Becca can heal the scars no one else sees. Desire is the easy part. Love is as hard as it gets. Good thing Nick is always up for a challenge...

Hard As You Can (Hard Ink #2)

Ever since hard-bodied, drop-dead-charming Shane McCallan strolled into the dance club where Crystal Dean works, he's shown a knack for getting beneath her defenses. For her little sister's sake, Crystal can't get too close. Until her job and Shane's mission intersect, and he reveals talents that go deeper than she could have guessed.

Shane McCallan doesn't turn his back on a friend in need, especially a former Special Forces teammate running a dangerous, off-the-books operation. Nor can he walk away from Crystal. The gorgeous blonde waitress is hiding secrets she doesn't want him to uncover. Too bad. He's exactly the man she needs to protect her sister, her life, and her heart. All he has to do is convince her that when something feels this good, you hold on as hard as you can—and never let go.

Hard to Hold On To (Hard Ink #2.5)

Edward "Easy" Cantrell knows better than most the pain of not being able to save those he loves—which is why he is not going to let Jenna Dean out of his sight. He may have just met her, but

Jenna's the first person to make him feel alive since that devastating day in the desert more than a year ago.

Jenna has never met anyone like Easy. She can't describe how he makes her feel—and not just because he saved her life. No, the stirrings inside her stretch *far* beyond gratitude.

As the pair are thrust together while chaos reigns around them, they both know one thing: the things in life most worth having are the hardest to hold on to.

Hard to Come By (Hard Ink #3)

Caught between desire and loyalty...

Derek DiMarzio would do anything for the members of his disgraced Special Forces team—sacrifice his body, help a former teammate with a covert operation to restore their honor, and even go behind enemy lines. He just never expected to want the beautiful woman he found there.

When a sexy stranger asks questions about her brother, Emilie Garza is torn between loyalty to the brother she once idolized and fear of the war-changed man he's become. Derek's easy smile and quiet strength tempt Emilie to open up, igniting the desire between them and leading Derek to crave a woman he shouldn't trust.

As the team's investigation reveals how powerful their enemies are, Derek and Emilie must prove where their loyalties lie before hearts are broken and lives are lost. Because love is too hard to come by to let slip away...

Hard to Be Good (Hard Ink #3.5)

Hard Ink Tattoo owner Jeremy Rixey has taken on his brother's stateside fight against the forces that nearly killed Nick and his Special Forces team a year before. Now, Jeremy's whole world has been turned upside down—not the least of which by a brilliant, quiet blond man who tempts Jeremy to settle down for the first time ever.

Recent kidnapping victim Charlie Merritt has always been better with computers than people, so when he's drawn into the SF team's investigation of his army colonel father's corruption, he's surprised to find acceptance and friendship—especially since his father *never* accepted who Charlie was. Even more surprising is the heated tension Charlie feels with sexy, tattooed Jeremy, Charlie's opposite in almost every way.

With tragedy and chaos all around them, temptation flashes hot, and Jeremy and Charlie can't help but wonder why they're trying so hard to be good...

Hard to Let Go (Hard Ink #4)

Beckett Murda hates to dwell on the past. But his investigation into the ambush that killed half his Special Forces team and ended his Army career gives him little choice. Just when his team learns how powerful their enemies are, hard-ass Beckett encounters the biggest complication yet—seductive, feisty Katherine Rixey.

A tough, stubborn prosecutor, Kat visits her brothers' Hard Ink Tattoo following a bad break-up—and finds herself staring down the barrel of a stranger's gun. Beckett is hard-bodied and sexy as hell, but he's also the most infuriating man *ever*. Worse, Kat's brothers are at war with criminals her office is investigating. When Kat joins the fight, she lands straight in Beckett's sights—and his arms. Not to mention their enemies' crosshairs.

Now Beckett and Kat must set aside their differences to work together, because finding love is never easy, and getting justice is hard to the end...

THE HEROES SERIES

Her Forbidden Hero (Heroes #1)

She's always been off-limits...

Former Army Special Forces Sgt. Marco Vieri has never thought of Alyssa Scott as more than his best friend's little sister, but her return home changes that...and challenges him to keep his war-borne demons at bay. Marco's not the same person he was back when he protected Alyssa from her abusive father, and he's not about to let her see the mess he's become.

...but now she's all grown up.

When Alyssa takes a job at the bar where Marco works, her carefree smiles wreak havoc on his resolve to bury his feelings. How can he protect her when he can't stop thinking about her in his bed? But Alyssa's not looking for protection— not anymore. Now that she's back in his life, she's determined to heal her forbidden hero, one touch at a time...

One Night with a Hero (Heroes #2)

He wants just one night...

After growing up with an abusive, alcoholic father, Army Special Forces Sgt. Brady Scott vowed never to marry or have kids. Sent stateside to get his head on straight—and his anger in check—Brady's looking for a distraction.

He finds it in his beautiful new neighbor's one-night-only offer for hot sex, but her ability to make him forget is addictive. Suddenly, Brady's not so sure he can stay away.

...what they need is each other.

Orphaned as a child, community center director Joss Daniels swore she'd never put herself in a position to be left behind again, but she can't deny herself one sizzling night with the sexy soldier who makes her laugh and kisses her senseless. When Joss discovers she's pregnant, Brady's rejection leaves her feeling abandoned. Now, they must overcome their fears before they lose the love and security they've found in each other, but can they let go of the past to create a future together?

ABOUT THE AUTHOR

Laura Kaye is the New York Times and USA Today bestselling author of nearly twenty books in contemporary and paranormal romance. Laura grew up amid family lore involving angels, ghosts, and evil-eye curses, cementing her life-long fascination with storytelling and the supernatural. Laura lives in Maryland with her husband, two daughters, and cute-but-bad dog, and appreciates her view of the Chesapeake Bay every day.

Visit Laura Kaye at
www.LauraKayeAuthor.com
Follow Laura on Twitter at
@LauraKayeAuthor
Like **LauraKayeWrites** on Facebook

Manufactured by Amazon.ca
Acheson, AB

12898445R00067